Beezle's Bravery

by

Joey Elliott

It was late afternoon in Dry Bay, Alaska. The faraway
mountains were golden and the melting spring snow glistened.
Long, purple shadows reached from the trees toward the river,
like slender fingers.

At the edge of the forest were two moose, a mother and her yearling calf. The mother was munching on tender shoots of birch and alder. Beezle, the calf, was playing with her shadow.

Often she had watched her tall, graceful mother fade into the dark brush like mist. One minute she would be there—the very next, she would be gone, dark against dark, and still.

Beezle stepped smoothly into a blue shadow. She felt the cool air against her bristly coat. From somewhere nearby a long howl drifted through the trees. "O-w-oooo." The hairs in Beezle's long mane stood on end. Her ears went back. She shivered.

"Beezle, you must not jump each time a wolf howls," her mother said. "You are a yearling now. You are five times the size of the biggest wolf. Wolves attack only the sick moose, or the very young calf. You must learn to act calm and show no weakness. No wolf will bother you if you know you are strong."

"But I do not know I am strong," replied Beezle. "I know you are strong. Thank goodness you are here to protect me."

"Shall I tell her now?" wondered her mother.

Just then a branch snapped. Beezle danced with fright. But it was only a young bull moose, peering nearsightedly around a bush. Soft fur, called velvet, covered his stubby antlers. In the fall, he would lose this velvet covering, and his antlers would shine. He would rub them against trees, and bang them against the antlers of other bulls. But now the young antlers were tender. He moved his head slowly, to protect them.

4

He stared at Beezle for a long moment. "This is where I browse," his eyes seemed to say. He glared. His dewlap moved from side to side as he swayed on his long legs.

"There is plenty for all," Beezle's mother snorted. And she stared right back. Soon he wandered off. Beezle and her mother went back to browsing on buds and sprouts.

As the last light faded, Beezie and her mother moved into the forest. Near a thick cover of highbush cranberry, they found a soft place to bed down for the night. They lay down, and began to rechew the afternoon meal. They took a long time on each mouthful of cud, chewing the pulp fine and swallowing it.

Farther up the river, two wolves were waking up in their den. One was unusually large, with thick, black fur. The other was his mate, and she was smaller and a light gray color. She stretched her forelegs out along the smooth floor of the den, her rump high in the air. She wagged her tail, and leaned over to lick the dark wolf's nose. The black wolf licked her back.

The two wolves crept out of the entrance to their den. White birds huddled down against the snow, unmoving. Their feathers made them almost invisible, so the wolves did not spot them. A pale moon drifted up from the treetops. Moonlight fell over the sparkling snow, turning it blue. The big wolf lifted his nose into the crisp air. "O-w-ooooooo," he howled.

Several young wolves emerged from the woods. These were pack members, with nearby dens of their own. They trusted the strength of the large leader and his mate, and they hunted together. They moved forward, their bellies low to the ground, approaching the leader. One by one, they touched noses, wagging their tails.

For a while the wolves were playful. They jumped on each other, frisking and chasing in the moonlight. One of the younger wolves snapped at the leader's mate, in mischief. Instantly she corrected him with a growl and a flash of white teeth. He rolled over onto his back, his tail curled between his legs. She put her nose in the air, and pranced away.

The leader began to bay again. The other wolves joined in, blending their long, sad howls. The song drifted over the snow. "Soon we will hunt," the song seemed to say. The leader began to trot quickly across the snow. His mate ran just behind his waving tail. The others fell into line. The wolves floated silently as smoke along the river bank.

Downriver, Beezle's mother stopped chewing her cud. She lifted her keen nose, and listened. "Wolf," she said, sniffing the crisp air. "I smell wolf. Stand up, Beezle."

Beezle jumped to her hooves, skittering with alarm. "<u>No</u>, Beezle. Be calm," said her mother firmly. "Stay quiet. And stay behind me."

From around the highbush cranberry came the dark wolf, moving slowly on silent paws. His pale eyes found Beezle's mother. One by one the other wolves moved to his side. They watched the two moose. Beezle shivered. But Beezle's mother never budged. Tall and sure, she just looked at the black wolf.

The leader looked at Beezle. She was a large calf—but still, a calf. If he could separate the two. . . But then he looked at Beezle's mother. Her eyes never left the big wolf's eyes. She stared down at him from her great height.

"Just try it," her eyes seemed to be saying. "Just try it, if you wish to be cut to ribbons."

And slowly, the wolves lowered their eyes. Slowly, they turned and moved away. Their dark fur melted into the black of the forest.

"How could you be so <u>brave</u>?" asked Beezle. "I was never so frightened. I wanted to run away."

Beezle's mother sighed. "Beezle, you can run very fast. But you cannot outrun a wolf. You must learn to act as big and as brave as you look. And you must learn it soon. For very soon you will be on your own. Very soon I must leave you, Beezle, for I must care for a new calf." She sighed again. "Or twins," she added thoughtfully. "I have a feeling it will be twins this time."

"But who will keep me safe from grizzlies and wolves?" bleated Beezle.

"<u>You</u> will keep you safe," replied her mother.

"But when I was on my own, I almost drowned," said Beezle, nearly crying. "I fell on the ice. I hurt myself. I didn't keep myself safe. You had to save me. And I learned never to go off on my own."

"You were younger then, Beezle," said the cow. "All moose go off on their own as they get older. It is the way of moose to be alone."

Beezle looked sadly at her mother, trying to understand. "But I will be so sad," she whispered.

"At first," said her mother. "But you will find the sadness goes in a few days. And in its place comes a new kind of joy. There is a real delight in being alone, in being a moose. Listen. I will sing you the song of the moose, as my mother sang it to me:

Fade as silently as fog
Deep into a forest haven.
Swim in the silver light of lake
Under the wheeling gull and raven.
Lift long legs through crusted snow—
None will hinder where you go.
For a moose, once fully grown,
Goes alone. Goes alone.

Beezle was silent, as the last of the song faded. Then she asked, "Must you go soon?"

"Very soon. But you will have the sky and the tall trees to keep you company."

"I am glad you are here now," said Beezle. "I am glad you keep me company."

For the next few weeks, Beezle stayed very close to her mother. No wolf came again to disturb the quiet spring days. Her mother and Beezle found new shoots of eelgrass growing in the river. At night they bedded under the whispering branches in the forest, and chewed their cuds in peace.

But one morning Beezle's mother told her it was time. Beezle did not want to go. At first she tried to follow her mother. But her mother was firm.

"The time for new calves is here. I cannot argue, Beezle. It is time for you to grow up. Remember the song, and go alone."

Beezle put her face against her mother's warm fur for a moment. Then she turned and trotted away.

For days, Beezle wandered. She did not feel like eating. She stared at the river, not seeing it. There seemed to be a gray mist in her mind. She felt dull, and heavy. Being alone felt strange. She missed her gentle mother. She missed the sound of her mother's chewing at night. She missed the warmth of another body nearby.

But as the days moved along, the dull feeling gave way to other feelings. She began to notice how the sun sparkled on the river. Beezle would plunge into the icy water and swim a long way. She found juicy chokeberry growing along the banks. Each one seemed to burst in her mouth with sweetness. The wind sang to her each day. An owl called at night.

One day Beezle realized that she had followed the river all the way to the ocean. A seagull called from high above. A splash drew her eyes to the water.

"What a nose," said a familiar voice. "It grows and grows."

"Scamp," yelled Beezle, spotting the sea otter. "I am so glad to see you."

"Where is your mother?" asked Scamp.

"She has a new calf or two by now," said Beezle, proud that her voice did not tremble. "A moose once grown goes alone, you know."

But Scamp was not paying attention. "See that snow?" he said. "Where's it go?" Scamp loved to make rhymes. Beezle laughed. But she looked where his eyes were peering, and saw a small cloud of snow moving fast in their direction. Quickly it grew larger. And from the cloud came a furry, white snowshoe hare with long, black-tipped ears.

"Frolic," said Beezle and Scamp, together.

"No time to talk," said Frolic. "Wolves are coming. Coming fast. Run, Beezle." And Frolic leaped sideways, and bounded off across the snow.

Beezle turned around to look. Sure enough, here were the wolves she had met earlier. At the head of the pack she could see the dark fur of the leader. On they came, closer and closer. They never even seemed to see the small, white snowshoe hare, who was disappearing in the distance.

"Jump," said Scamp. "Jump into the water." But Beezle did not jump. For the icy banks were steep and broken. If she jumped, she might never get ashore. She stood very still as the wolves circled around.

The wolves snarled and growled at Beezle. They lunged at her legs, then drew back. But Beezle did not budge. She was remembering her mother's words. Her days alone had given her new courage. She seemed to know just what to do.

As the leader jumped at Beezle's belly, Beezle reared into the air. She lashed out with her sharp front hooves. With a yelp, the lead wolf ducked away. But now his mate jumped for Beezle's rump. Beezle saw her coming. She lifted her hind hooves, and tossed the wolf into a drift. The stunned wolf lay there, whining softly.

Another wolf moved in close, snapping at Beezle's legs. But Beezle seemed to be everywhere at once. She struck out with her forelegs. She kicked out with her hind hooves. And one by one, the wolves fell back.

The leader held her eyes with his own. "You have grown strong," he seemed to be saying. "But there may come another day. Do not forget me."

And he turned to limp away over the snow. His pack followed
behind him.

"What a fight," said Scamp, doing a backflip dive. "What a
sight."

But Beezle said nothing. She watched as the last gray wolf
disappeared in the distance. She lifted her head high.

"You were so brave, Beezle," Scamp said. "How did you become
so brave?"

"It is the way of moose," said Beezle.

"It is not _my_ way," responded Scamp. "I am glad to be a sea
otter." And he dove, in search of a spiny sea urchin or a clam.

"But I am glad to be a moose," said Beezle softly. She watched the ripples left by Scamp's dive. She felt the breeze from the sea ruffle her coat. The salty air smelled fresh and clean. She remembered the words of her mother's song. Silently, she added a verse of her own:

> Gull and tree and shimmering sea
> Are all I need for company.

To Stuart N. Houk, who supplied the inspiration.

The author gratefully acknowledges the technical assistance of Lowell Suring, of the Department of Wildlife and Fisheries in Alaska, and Dr. Charles Handley of The Smithsonian Institution.

Points of Interest in This Book

p. 1. Alsek River, Dry Bay, Alaska
p. 5. "dewlap": the bell that hangs from the underjaw of an adult moose, longer on bulls
p. 8. wolves in den
p. 7. highbush cranberry
p. 23. a snowshoe hare; a sea otter

Text copyright © 1989 by Soundprints Corporation and The Smithsonian Institution. Illustrations copyright © 1989 by Soundprints Corporation, a subsidiary of Trudy Corporation, 165 Water Street, Norwalk, CT 06856. Manufactured by Horowitz/Rae Book Manufacturers, Inc. Designed by Judy Oliver, Oliver and Lake Design Associates. First edition 10 9 8 7 6 5 4 3 2 1.

Library of Congress Cataloging-in-Publications Data
Elliott, Joey   Beezle's Bravery
Summary: A moose yearling living near the Alsek River in Alaska learns through her experiences that she has developed sufficient strength and self-confidence to leave her mother and live on her own.
1. Moose—juvenile literature   [1. Moose]
1. Elliott, Joey.   11. Title.
ISBN: 0-924483-17-2